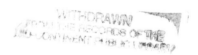

Dear Parents and Educators,

Welcome to Penguin Young Readers! As parents and educators, you know that each child develops at his or her own pace—in terms of speech, critical thinking, and, of course, reading. Penguin Young Readers recognizes this fact. As a result, each Penguin Young Readers book is assigned a traditional easy-to-read level (1–4) as well as a Guided Reading Level (A–P). Both of these systems will help you choose the right book for your child. Please refer to the back of each book for specific leveling information. Penguin Young Readers features esteemed authors and illustrators, stories about favorite characters, fascinating nonfiction, and more!

Batman: The Brave and the Bold
Day of the Dark Knight!

LEVEL 4

GUIDED READING LEVEL **N**

This book is perfect for a **Fluent Reader** who:
- can read the text quickly with minimal effort;
- has good comprehension skills;
- can self-correct (can recognize when something doesn't sound right); and
- can read aloud smoothly and with expression.

Here are some **activities** you can do during and after reading this book:
- Identify the problem in the story.
- There are many characters in this story. On a separate sheet of paper, make a list of all the characters. Which ones are good characters? Which ones are bad? Explain why.
- Make Predictions: Will Batman be *The One Who Is Worthy*?

Remember, sharing the love of reading with a child is the best gift you can give!

—Bonnie Bader, EdM, and Katie Carella, EdM
   Penguin Young Readers program

*Penguin Young Readers are leveled by independent reviewers applying the standards developed by Irene Fountas and Gay Su Pinnell in *Matching Books to Readers: Using Leveled Books in Guided Reading*, Heinemann, 1999.

Penguin Young Readers
Published by the Penguin Group
Penguin Group (USA) Inc., 375 Hudson Street, New York, New York 10014, USA
Penguin Group (Canada), 90 Eglinton Avenue East, Suite 700,
Toronto, Ontario M4P 2Y3, Canada (a division of Pearson Penguin Canada Inc.)
Penguin Books Ltd., 80 Strand, London WC2R 0RL, England
Penguin Group Ireland, 25 St. Stephen's Green, Dublin 2, Ireland (a division of Penguin Books Ltd.)
Penguin Group (Australia), 250 Camberwell Road, Camberwell, Victoria 3124,
Australia (a division of Pearson Australia Group Pty. Ltd.)
Penguin Books India Pvt. Ltd., 11 Community Centre, Panchsheel Park, New Delhi—110 017, India
Penguin Group (NZ), 67 Apollo Drive, Rosedale, Auckland 0632, New Zealand
(a division of Pearson New Zealand Ltd.)
Penguin Books (South Africa) (Pty.) Ltd., 24 Sturdee Avenue, Rosebank,
Johannesburg 2196, South Africa

Penguin Books Ltd., Registered Offices: 80 Strand, London WC2R 0RL, England

The publisher does not have any control over and does not assume any responsibility
for author or third-party websites or their content.

ISBN 978-0-448-45719-2   10 9 8 7 6 5 4 3 2 1

BATMAN
THE BRAVE AND THE BOLD

DAY OF THE
DARK KNIGHT!

adapted by Jade Ashe
based on the teleplay by J. M. DeMatteis
Batman created by Bob Kane

Penguin Young Readers
An Imprint of Penguin Group (USA) Inc.

Batman and his friend Green Arrow were on the scene at a prison break. The heroes were trying to stop the prisoners from escaping.

A prisoner with long, white hair and a
beard appeared before them. Batman
tossed a Batarang and Green Arrow
shot an arrow to stop him from escaping.
The prisoner began to speak.

"Bend, time, bend . . . then rip
apart . . . carry us back to home
and heart."

Light appeared around him. In a
flash, the prisoner was gone—and so
were Batman and Green Arrow.

The next thing they knew, they were all standing in an open field. Green Arrow aimed an arrow at the prisoner. "Where are we?" he asked.

"It is the fifth century AD. The place is Britain, and I am Merlin," the prisoner responded.

Merlin explained that the kingdom of
Camelot had been overthrown by King
Arthur's half sister, Morgaine le Fey.
She had turned all of Camelot's subjects
into stone, including King Arthur.

Merlin created an image in the sky of the sword Excalibur.

"Only Excalibur's magic can defeat le Fey and restore our king," Merlin said.

"Then why haven't you used it?" Batman asked.

"Only *The One Who Is Worthy* can retrieve it," Merlin replied.

In the throne room of the castle,
Morgaine le Fey watched Merlin and
the two heroes through a magical
mirror.

"Merlin must not be allowed to
retrieve the sword," Morgaine said to
her servant, Jason Blood.

Morgaine le Fey began to chant.
"Change! Change, oh form of man!
Release thy might from fleshy mire! Boil
thy blood in heart of fire!"

Her servant's body began to change into the form of a demon named Etrigan. With the change complete, the demon left the castle in search of Merlin and the two heroes.

Merlin explained why he brought the heroes to Camelot.

"I turned to magic to reveal the one person in all of the universe—besides Arthur himself—who could free the sword from the stone. It is clear that you, my Dark Knight, are our shining hope," Merlin said.

Suddenly Etrigan and a team of monstrous Knightbeasts burst up through the ground and toppled Batman's horse. Batman scrambled to his feet just as the demon tried to attack him.

Merlin cast a spell that knocked
Etrigan to the ground.

"You were my servant once, before
Morgaine stole you, and you shall be
my servant again!" Merlin yelled.

Etrigan appeared behind Merlin and
knocked him over.

Etrigan looked at Batman and Green
Arrow.

He created a magical wave of flames
that he breathed at the heroes as he
fled through the forest.

After the battle, Merlin and the two heroes made their way to the Tower of Excalibur.

"The time has come for you to enter the tower and remove the sword from the stone," Merlin said to Batman.

Suddenly two ogres rose out of the water surrounding the tower.

"Only *The One Who Is Worthy* can defeat the ogres," Merlin said.

One of the ogres grabbed Green
Arrow. He fired a Sonic Arrow at
the ogre and fell to the ground as it
exploded. The ogre was knocked out.

Batman took out the second ogre by putting two pellets from his Utility Belt into its nose. The pellets exploded! The ogre was defeated.

After the heroes' victory, the water surrounding the tower swirled and magically created a bridge leading from the beach to the tower's gate.

"The spirits of the tower have seen your victory, Dark Knight," Merlin said to Batman.

"You may now enter and retrieve Excalibur," Merlin said.

"Not just yet, Merlin," a voice rang out.

Morgaine le Fey and Etrigan appeared behind Merlin and the two heroes.

"Excalibur's magic rules here, Morgaine. No sorcery can prevent Batman from reaching his destiny," Merlin said.

"I have no intention of stopping him," Morgaine said.

Her eyes glowed.

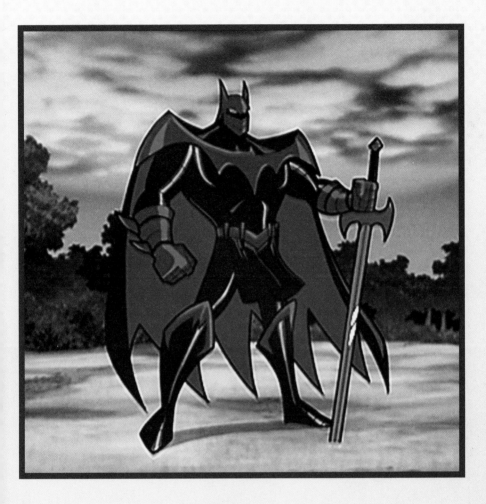

"I *want* him to reach his destiny," she
continued, "so he may gain Excalibur
for his new master!"

Black armor suddenly covered
Batman, and his eyes glowed red. He
was under Morgaine's control!

Batman raced up the tower while
Merlin fought Morgaine and Etrigan.

"Here is a chance to prove yourself!"
Merlin said to Green Arrow.

Green Arrow followed Batman.

Green Arrow leaped in front of Batman.

"C'mon, Bats. You're not gonna let her dance you around like a puppet, are you?" Green Arrow said as he fought Batman.

Batman and Green Arrow reached
the edge of a cliff. Green Arrow fell,
but quickly grabbed the ledge. Batman
stepped on Green Arrow's hand.

"Easy, Bats! Easy!" Green Arrow said to Batman. "It's me, your buddy."

The spell holding Batman started to fade.

"Green Arrow?" he said.

Morgaine appeared behind Batman.

"Destroy him!" she said to the Caped Crusader.

Batman kicked his friend and watched as Green Arrow fell from the cliff into the mist below.

Back at the bottom of the cliff, Merlin
and Etrigan fought.

"Change! Change, oh form of man!"
Merlin chanted.

A ball of energy shot to the tower.

Morgaine started to lead Batman into the hall holding Excalibur. Merlin's ball of energy hit Batman in the back. He grunted behind Morgaine.

"What is it?" she asked.

"Nothing," he said.

Morgaine and Batman entered the
hall and saw Excalibur.

"Fulfill your destiny, Dark Knight.
Remove the sword from the stone,"
Morgaine said.

Batman approached the sword, but quickly turned around to toss an explosive Batarang at Morgaine. The spell had been lifted.

"How?" Morgaine screamed.

Merlin and Morgaine's servant, Jason
Blood, appeared in the hall.

"Merlin has released me from your
spell. He has given me my freedom,"
Blood said.

"What good is freedom to the dead?"
Morgaine screamed at Jason.

Her body began to change into a
giant dragon. The dragon flew to the
top of the tower, laughing.

"Excalibur! It's our only chance,"
Merlin yelled to Batman.

Batman ran to the sword and tried to
remove it from the stone.

"It. Won't. Come. Out!" Batman said, struggling with the sword.

"Then . . . you're not *The One Who Is Worthy*?" Merlin asked.

The dragon swatted at Batman.
Jason Blood willingly turned into
Etrigan to battle the dragon. He roared
a wave of flame at the beast, who shot
back flames of her own.

Merlin used his spells, Batman shot grenades, and Etrigan continued his fire attack. The dragon threw herself against the tower. The entire tower started to collapse.

"Arthur's reign is done and you with
it!" the dragon said.

Etrigan leaped toward the dragon,
but the dragon used her powers to turn
him and Merlin to stone. She turned
toward Batman to finish the battle.

Suddenly an arrow flew into the
dragon's head. Green Arrow appeared.
"You think your arrows can stop me?"
the dragon roared.

"Maybe not," Green Arrow said. "But I'm betting *this* will!"

Green Arrow grabbed Excalibur, but the sword did not budge.

"Only *The One Who Is Worthy* can release the sword from the stone. All you are worthy of is failure and death!" Morgaine cried.

Batman approached Green Arrow
and the stone.

"Maybe," Batman said, "the *one* who
is worthy is really *two*."

Batman and Green Arrow both
grabbed Excalibur.

The two heroes pulled Excalibur from the stone together. Batman handed the sword to Green Arrow. He shot the sword at Morgaine. It hit her in the heart.

Blinding light covered them all as Morgaine screamed. She was gone.

"I misjudged you, Archer," Merlin said to Green Arrow.

Etrigan left the three men in a swirl of smoke.

Merlin and the two heroes headed
back to Camelot.

"King Arthur will be most grateful
for all you have done," Merlin said to
Batman and Green Arrow.

Merlin cast a final spell over the
two heroes. Batman and Green Arrow
found themselves back in Gotham.
Another job well done.